This book belongs to:

· ·

For my Pappy
Petunias still bloom for you, as do I.
My fondest love.

Thanks Stephen, and Theo.

E.H

The Little Gardener © Flying Eye Books 2015.

This is a first paperback edition published in 2017 by Flying Eye Books,
an imprint of Nobrow Ltd. 27 Westgate Street, London E8 3RL.

Text and illustrations © Emily Hughes 2015.
Emily Hughes has asserted her right under the Copyright,
Designs and Patents Act, 1988, to be identified as the
Author and Illustrator of this Work.

2 4 6 8 10 9 7 5 3 1

Published in the US by Nobrow (US) Inc.
Printed in Poland on on FSC® certified paper
ISBN: 978-1-911171-24-9

Order from www.flyingeyebooks.com

The Little Gardener

Emily Hughes

Flying Eye Books

London - New York

This was the garden.

It didn't look like much,

but it meant everything to its gardener.

It was his home. It was his supper.

It was his joy.

Only, he wasn't much good at gardening.

It wasn't that he didn't work hard.

He worked hard,

very, very hard.

He was just too little.

But there was one thing that did blossom in his garden.

It was a flower.

It was alive and wonderful.

It gave the gardener hope and
it made him work even harder.

He worked all morning.
He worked all afternoon.

He worked all night.

Still, the garden was dying.

He would have no home.
He would have no supper.

He would have no joy.

One night, feeling tired and sad, he made a wish.

—I wish I had a bit of help

No one heard his little voice,

but someone saw his flower.

It was alive and wonderful.

It gave the someone hope.
It made the someone want to work harder.

The next day the gardener was weary and slept the whole day.

He slept the whole week. He slept the whole month.

And when he finally awoke,

it had been just long enough for something to change.

This is the garden now.

And this is its gardener.

He doesn't look like much,
but he means everything to his garden.

Love this book?
Check out *Wild*

*No one remembered how she came to the woods,
but all knew it was right.*

The brilliant debut picture book by Emily Hughes tells
the story of a little girl who is unabashedly, irrefutably,
irrepressibly *Wild*. That is, until one day she meets
a new animal that looks oddly like her...

Order from www.flyingeyebooks.com or all good bookshops
ISBN: 978-1-909263-62-8